Mystery of the Asteroid Belt

Safaa A. Mhawi

Mystery of the Asteroid Belt
Copyright © 2020 by S.A.M. Safaa A. Mhawi

Library of Congress Control Number: 2020913614
ISBN-13: Paperback: 978-1-64749-195-6
          epub   978-1-64749-196-3

All rights reserved. No part of this publication may be reproduced, distributed, or transmitted in any form or by any means, including photocopying, recording, or other electronic or mechanical methods, without the prior written permission of the publisher or author, except in the case of brief quotations embodied in critical reviews and certain other noncommercial uses permitted by copyright law.

Although every precaution has been taken to verify the accuracy of the information contained herein, the author and publisher assume no responsibility for any errors or omissions.No liability is assumed for damages that may result from the use of information contained within.

Printed in the United States of America

GoToPublish LLC
1-888-337-1724
www.gotopublish.com
info@gotopublish.com

Contents

Dedication vii
Thankfulness Appreciation ix
Introduction xi
Chapter One 1
Chapter Two 7
Chapter Three 11
Chapter Four 17
Chapter Five 23
Chapter Six 29
Chapter Seven 33
Chapter Eight 37
Chapter Nine 39
Chapter Ten 43
Chapter Eleven 47
Chapter Twelve 51
Chapter Thirteen 59
Chapter Fourteen 69
Chapter Fifteen 79
Chapter Sixteen 85

Dedication

To my wonderful wife.

If you were not with me, the world would not know me as a writer.

Initials
S.A.M
Safaa Abdlhuassein Mhawi

Thankfulness Appreciation

To the translators
Ryadh Al-Mandiwi & Baha Muhawi

The Proofreader
Juliana Garcia

And
Cover designer.
The artist
Rafi Al Haidar

Introduction

In the beginning, I would like to send you the warmest greetings. I thank you for choosing to read my book; it is my first work. I chose to write about science fiction, as what we now know as science, was once consider myths and legends. One day, what you will read in this book is what you might see in the near future with your own eyes. There are a lot of writers in this field (science fiction, and prediction of scientific discoveries); the most famous is Jules Verne, the father of the art of science fiction.

Writing this story took eighteen months; I wanted to give you a beautiful, coherent, and exciting story, as much as possible.

I hope I was successful in that.

Thank you for your time.

Safaa Mhawi

Chapter One

The story is born from the theories of the asteroid belt formation, which is located in the area between the planets Mars and Jupiter.

The story begins with sending a space expedition to the asteroid belt led by the famous astronaut Jacob Brown; —a man in the middle of the third decade of his life smart, with amazing acumen.

When planning this expedition, NASA wants to send the best astronaut they have. NASA created a program that would allow the main computer to choose a match for the expedition from the seven thousand astronauts they have. The computer chooses Captain Jacob Brown with a match of 89 percent.

Captain Jacob is indescribably happy when NASA chooses him for this mission. He has his personal reasons for this happiness. Since his childhood, Jacob was dedicated to space and specifically to that mysterious area of the solar system which is called the asteroid belt.

Before mankind entered the space age, there wasn't a lot of information available except from watching and basic monitoring of the solar system and its planets with all their moons that follow these planets. When humanity entered the age of laser and giant telescopes and the detector spectroscopy, a very wide holistic view about the solar system was gained. has They even obtained the composition of the very distant planet's soil by using the x-ray spectroscopy scouts.

All these space theories were cleared and understandable except the theory of the asteroid belt. This theory was saying that the asteroid belt was created from the remains of a small planet that was orbiting Jupiter, because the huge gravitational force of Jupiter was caused by the different size of the two planets. That led to the small planet to gravitate toward Jupiter where it was completely destroyed; its pieces scattered in the form of rocks with different sizes that made an asteroid belt nomad between Mars and Jupiter. "This is not true and totally illogical." That's what Mr. Brown, the grandfather, was repeating on the ears of the young Jacob. Mr. Brown was an archaeologist and professor in one of Boston's Universities; he specialized in the study of ancient and extinct civilizations.

When junior Jacob was asking his grandfather about the universe and how it works, the grandfather was answering the following: the general order of the universe is a different configuration of space objects, planets, stars, meteors, rocks, and all these configurations have their own specific geostationary orbit, which they spin in on a regular basis.

There was a small planet between Jupiter and Mars but it was not destroyed because of Jupiter's gravity and that's for two reasons.

"But what destroyed that planet, Grandpa?" Jacob asked his grandfather.

"I don't know exactly, but I refuse the idea that the planet was destroyed because of gravity, as I told you for two reasons. First: each luminary has a specific orbit; therefore, it cannot budge from its place, only with a tremendous force. The second reason is the great distance between that planet and Jupiter.

The proof is, if the distance between those two planets was close, the asteroid belt would have completely disappeared by being pulled to the atmosphere of Jupiter and that would turn it to meteoroids and meteor showers on the surface of Jupiter or Mars. Something terrible had happened in that deep time that destroyed the planet. I believe there was a very highly advanced civilization on it, as I am sure the coming days will reveal the truth."

In these days, Mr. Brown was on the verge of revealing a big and very important discovery after he found an ancient artifact in Peru after fifteen years of exploration, together with a crew of ancient artifacts specialists. He came out with amazing conclusions about connections between the old civilizations on Earth and other very advanced civilizations from outer space.

What reinforced Mr. Brown's theory was that he found a manuscript in the king's room. That manuscript contained a map of an airport. After they translated the words on the bottom of the map, these words were GODDESS AIRSTRIP.

There was also some kind of vehicle in that airport but it had a different shape from the other ordinary vehicles in the courtyard of the royal palace and the other parts of the city. In the upper right scheme of the solar system with all the planets was a small planet between Jupiter and Mars. That was what really reinforced Mr. Brown's theory about a connection between space creatures and the people on Earth.

So, as we said, Mr. Brown was about to reveal his great discovery to the scientific circles and all about the manuscript. However, after a close inspection of the old manuscript, he found that there was a missing part. He had a couple of thoughts about the place of the other part of the manuscript but he couldn't find it. All that he found was exploration equipment that was from a not too far period of time which was around 200 or 300 years ago, the same time of the Spanish expeditions.

When he revealed his theory, it didn't receive great acceptance from the researchers in that field and they said to Mr. Brown: "We do appreciate your painstaking effort through your search for the past fifteen years… But where is the conclusive evidence that proves the information in the manuscript is correct? Maybe that was some imagination of an artist or idea that was introduced to the king in that time or a part of a sacred book, who knows? And don't forget the missing part of this manuscript; maybe it has more and better evidence that can confirm your theory."

It was a big shock to Mr. Brown because after all that hard work with all the efforts he made, he couldn't reach his target. So he secluded his work, after having that big disappointment.

Little Jacob, who was very close to him, listened luxuriously for his stories of adventures in all discovery trips.

When Mr. Brown left the work of digging in his last days, young Jacob was accompanying him everywhere. Until one day, while they were watching a photography report on TV about the last discovery of space and the report was also talking about the asteroid belt.

Little Jacob was listening with interest for the explanation of the theory of the planetary belt's formation; meanwhile, his grandpa was filled with silence.

At the end of the report, young Jacob asked his grandfather: "What do you think happened there, grandpa?"

"I don't know exactly, my child, but I told you there was a planet with a great civilization that was destroyed because of a strong logical reason. I was about to prove all that with absolute scientific evidence, but the facts betrayed me my child."

"I will go there someday to see that asteroid belt by myself." That's what Jacob Brown was saying when he was a child.

All these memories were running in Captain Brown's head while his ship was roaming near the asteroid belt.

Chapter Two

"I will save the world someday." That was what Rebecca Z. Welch saying prove to herself.

She was a willowy girl with strong beautiful green eyes showing a sharp intelligence.

She was emerging of course, because she was the granddaughter of Welch Zuckerberg the great, the founder of the first antique store in Houston, Texas.

He started working in this business more than 200 years ago when he was a Youngman in the prime of his life; he loved traveling and adventures.

When his business flourished and expanded, he traveled to many countries bringing many ancient artifacts for different civilizations. So if you enter his store now you will find yourself in a real museum including artifacts from the east and west of the Earth.

Rebecca loved the adventures. She was very proud of her grandfather Big Welch. Thanks to him, the Welch antique stores were known with a distinct character in Texas and all of the U.S.

The life was monotonous and boring in these giant stores with a impossible challenge because the grandmother's rules, which she was always repeating: "I will never make a change in my father's store. He spent his life in these stores."

"But Grandma, the change is required." That was Rebecca's answer.

"No, I want to keep things the way I used to see and I don't want the place to lose the touch of my father."

"Grandma... please Okay, what about the leaks in the old side back of the building? The plumber said the old pipe was eaten by rust and we have to change it before it breaks and fills the basement with water. What do we need the OLD basement for any way?"

"I said NO, and instead of arguing with me, go down to the OLD basement and clean it so the plumber can see the pipe to fix it."

"WHAAAAT?" Rebecca screamed laughingly. "Is that my punishment? What have I done to be locked up in a basement more than 200 years old? Grandma... are you serious?"

The grandma gave a pointy look to Rebecca and said, "Aren't you looking for a new adventure? Go down to the old basement, clean it, and ANYTHING you find in that place is yours."

Rebecca liked the idea because this was not her first time to go down to the old basement, but this time she felt there was something hidden with a big adventure coming her way.

"All right, I accept," she said to her grandma.

The next day, Rebecca started the cleaning and repairing works.

This wasn't the first time she had seen the basement, which used to be considered the first storage room for the staff of Welch's great store.

The basement contained storage racks arranged in a regular shape to put the developed items on it that would be displayed in the shop's vitrines. Also there was a big table with cleaning equipment for cleaning the old artifacts and restoring them, if needed.

The basement also had a big iron safe with many small iron rooms that contained many racks and small lockers inside to keep the precious items.

Rebecca started cleaning from the far corners of the basement to the stairs moving the neglected stuff with all other dirt close to the stairs preparing it to be moved outside.

Two weeks later, the basement's condition got better and Rebecca was proud with her work. Her grandma was visiting her many times to encourage her to keep going. However, disappointment started getting to Rebecca about something special that could have appended... till she started moving the heavy items that's on the sides of the stairs.

One of the ancient pieces of rocks with a cylindrical shape belonging to a statue of an old pharos tended on the back side of the old stairs, breaking the wood shingles which cause a hole in the wall of the stairs.

Rebecca ran to the place of the fallen piece and moved it on the side to check the hole in the wall.

The wood was worn out and could be broken by hand. In the beginning, Rebecca was afraid to put her hand inside. However, she stopped herself fast she got a flash light to see inside.

Then she saw a leather bag inside the hole, but she had to expand the hole to get the bag out.

With a shaking hand, Rebecca moved the bag to the big table, but when she opened the bag, she had a big disappointment. The bag contained the manual of the big iron safe.

"Damn it, damn it." That's all that she said.

Chapter Three

"Sir... our navigation system indicates that we are approaching the cosmic area of the asteroid belt." That's what the navigation officer said to Captain Brown.

"Okay, gentlemen, the hour of work is here now, attention level C."

"Understood."

"Sensing sensors... ON."

"Infrared sensors... ON."

"Occupied satellite and navigation systems... ON."

"The crew will separate to two shifts for a week. After that, the work will be on three shifts, each shift works for eight hours." I will lead the first shift, then the second shift will be under the command of the first officer Mr. Joseph Condah. All the work will be distributed evenly—gentlemen, please pay a full attention to any small details and put it on records" That's how Captain Brown was giving his orders for his crew which they received a hard training for a long time on this mission.

"The target of this space expedition contains two parts. The first one is to reach the asteroid belt and discover its components. Secondly, establish a space base on one of the floating asteroids."

This idea was found by one of the well-known astronomers. It was simple, practical, with a fantastic strategic target.

The idea was to find some kind of a rocky space object to be the ground base of a multi-task space station.

First, this would save a lot of costs to bring materials to build that station.

Second, this space station would be the headquarter to discover the deep corners of the universe; space ships would lunch from that location and it would be the beginning of a new era for conquering the universe.

Work began in full swing to accomplish the expedition's targets, so they started a full scan of the components of the planetary system in addition to measuring the size of the asteroids in the belt and they found many encouraging results because some of these asteroids were real mines of many rare and valuable metals.

Captain Brown laughingly said: "That's great; these mines had covered the costs of our expedition and made all the crew members millionaires in a second! Keep your investment boys, but don't forget our target of this journey."

The crew started the hard work to implement the goals of the trip. After they scanned the area, the right asteroids had been chosen while NASA started sending the required materials to build the station by special ships designed for that purpose.

The crew found three asteroids that matched their requirements to start building the space station, but the most perfect asteroid among those three was the one Captain Brown called B 001 after his name.

"Let's take a close look on B 001." It was a strange asteroid for many reasons and it put the crew on hold for a while.

It was almost a regular spherical shape with a diameter of about 2000 meters, with different color from the rest of the asteroid belt.

Upon checking the components of B 001, they found it totally different from the rest of the system... the most strange thing about it was that it was free of cosmic radiation!

This was unique because.... the universe is fully loaded with the three cosmic rays: GAMMA, ALPHA, and BETA. These rays resulted from the atomic interactions of the sun and the other stars. These rays have a 100 percent killing effect on all kinds of life.

However, because of the great magnetic field around the Earth, you have full protection from these deadly radiations.

The strange thing about B 001 was that it did not have a magnetic field, but when they tried measuring the age of the planet, they found it dated back to 5,000,000 years ago!

During all these years, the cosmic radiations had no effect on the yellow soil of this asteroid so the scientists of Earth couldn't find explanation for the puzzle of B 001.

The scientists asked the crew to send a sample from B 001 for study purposes and after long study, they decided to choose B 001 to set up the space station. Therefore, they gave the orders to the crew to start the work on it.

The crew started the geological scan and the topographic survey for B 001 to locate digging spots on the asteroid. The scanning devices were floating around the "mini-planet" if we may say.

After few days of scanning, they found the right location for digging. Then, a new surprise appeared.

Through the digging process in one of the locations, the crew found a strange material body buried 10 meters below in the asteroid's surface.

The body had a ball shape almost with a flat base in the bottom, almost clear to the eye that you could almost see through. It looked like the body was made from a mixture of some metal and harsh rapper materials with a color close to gray.

The body surface contained many large holes organized and spread all over it except the base which didn't have any holes.

An excited got the crew while they were bringing the body inside the cockpit cabinet. They checked it with interest. There was some kind of control panel on the front, but it was turned off.

"What's that?" Capitan Brown asked with a calming voice. "Where did it come from? We are far from any visible civilizations so where did this thing come from? Alright, I want a full scan of this object; try to determine how old this thing is!"

The scanning came back with even more confusing results for the crew. The body was 5,000,000 years old and it didn't belong to our solar system. On the other hand, B 001 had the same age but it had the same material of the solar system and the asteroid belt.

"FOR GOD SAKE! What's that supposed to mean? The body and B 001 have the same age but different materials? Okay, how did this body end up inside B 001 in the first place and buried in it for all these millions of years? It's not even from the solar system? What happened here exactly? My grandpa was right, he was right, I will make another test and if the results come out positive, it means my anticipations with my grandpa's suspicions are in the right place."

The test required getting fifty samples from different asteroids of the belt, at a rate of two samples from each asteroid, one from the surface and the second from the depth.

After analyzing the two samples of each asteroid to find the age of each rock, the results came out the way Captain Brown expected.

The samples that were taken from the depth had the age of almost three billion years, but the samples from the surface had evidence of a change in the components because the cosmic radiations were dated back to 5,000,000 years ago.

"This confirms my intuition. There was a full planet here, three billion years old, but it turned into shattered pieces around 5,000,000 years ago. What happened here in that time? What's destroyed this planet? That's what we don't know." That was what Captain Brown said.

Captain Brown accomplished a bright success. He led the expedition with safety to the asteroid belt area, found a perfect location to set up a space station, plus all the mines he found in the asteroid belt.

So he decided to go back to Earth after two years away from our planet.

Captain Brown took back with him the strange body and two containers from the soil of B 001 with many other samples for research in NASA laboratories.

Chapter Four

After the adventure of cleaning the basement, boredom and routine were back in Rebecca's life. The plumber and his boys went to work to replace the broken pipe with a new one.

Additionally, they fixed the windows, and installed a new light system for the place that made it look so nice and clean.

The grandma was so glad with the new look of the basement and ascribed this change to Rebecca.

"Without my beautiful child, none of this would have ever happened."

She loved Rebecca so much because she was her favorite. "Sorry my dear if I make you tired."

"Please don't say that, Grandma, you know I want to see you smiling, always.

Life was back to the usual in great Zuckerberg stores until when that night while Rebecca stayed awake checking the store transactions.

The TV was on, but Rebecca didn't pay much attention to it. The TV was broadcasting a documentary report about the HAMILTON'S iron safes.

The HAMILTON Company was one of the very first companies in the iron industry with many products in this field.

One of the most famous products of this company was the iron safes; they started the job of iron safes designing more than 200 years ago.

Rebecca started listening with interest when the report on TV mentioned the HAMILTON safes, especially when it said that the company also designed safes based on their special customer's orders. Also there were some safes with a special design that contained secret drawers to hide valuable objects in.

Then a question jumped to Rebecca's mind: *Why does my grandpa hide the safe's manual?*

In seconds, Rebecca was in the basement browsing the manual. She didn't find anything exciting at first, and the manual showed how to install the safe and how to repair it.

At the end of the pages, Rebecca found some hand writing that said:

Don't let down your guard for friend or foe
let your spear ready 3and always up, not low,
signed by: the luck star.

What was that supposed to mean? Rebecca scratched her head wondering.

Rebecca went back to the safe with a small chair and flashlight. She sat inside the safe, and started checking the walls from the inside and the corners.

Then she noticed a solid body in the middle of the top part of the safe's gate from the inside.

The solid object was in the shape of a knight from the middle ages with a spear in his hand. The spear was pointing down.

Rebecca smiled and she said: "Okay Mr. Knight Guy, let's see what's happen if your spear points to the sky."

So she turned the spear up... But nothing happened. *Damn it! What is this stupid game? What is your puzzle, Grandpa?*

When she gathered up her mind, Rebecca remembered there was a star on the key of the safe. For some reason you could rotate that star in different directions.

After she pointed the spear up, she closed the safe's gate and locked it with the key, and then she rotated the star 180 degrees backward.

With a lot of excitement, she unlocked the gate with the key, turned it open, and pulled the gate.

Just as I expected! She was screaming with joy.

Rebecca expected that the spear was a switching device that could open a secret drawer inside the safe.

It was connected to the main mechanism inside the safe and when you rotated the star and repointed the spear up, you could open the secret drawer.

When she reopened the gate, there were bunches of drawers in the deep left side of the safe that had been moved forward making some kind a door.

She pulled the new door out to find more hidden drawers inside, but all that was inside was a middle sized box.

The box was made of wood with iron corners, not heavy without the lock; Rebecca pulled it out and put it on the big table in the basement.

Rebecca opened the box to find two pieces inside. The first piece was the shape of the sun, made from hard black material like stone or metal.

In the middle of the first piece, there was a dark red stone and it looked like it was on fire, like you could see the flame fingers coming out of the sun.

The second piece had a conical design, 10 centimeters in length, and on top of it was a weird replica of some bird.

To the back of this weird bird there was a tag attached to it. *With this tag, I can wear the mace of luck as a necklace.*

Mace of luck was what Rebecca called the second piece.

In the bottom of the box there was a piece of a very old, handwritten manuscript, the hand of the great Welch Zuckerberg himself.

Rebecca started reading:

> *I, Welch Zuckerberg, am writing these words to whom it may concern and to the person who will find this box after me.*

You need to know that I bought this box from two travelers, they had found the box in the remains of a Spanish convoy that came from South America. They told me the convoy was attacked by the red Indians and they were totally exterminated. The two travelers didn't see the battle but they figured it out by the evidence on the battle field. The red Indians took everything, wagons, ammo, foods, drinks, and tools. The travelers found the box under one of the destroyed wagons.

When they brought me the box, I could not find how old these pieces were, or where they came from. I also tried to translate the inscriptions from the ancient manuscript, but it didn't work with me.

The thing that really sparked my attention was: I couldn't find any match for those two pieces in any civilization I saw during my travels around world.

Even with all the countries that I visited in my journeys, nothing came even close to these two pieces. That's why I decided to keep them in the box. I had a weird and scary feeling about these pieces. And that made me hide the box in the secret drawer of the iron safe and not to put them for sale or any kind of trading business. The last thing that I am going to ask the next person who will find the box is DON'T MESS WITH THINGS BYOND OUR MINDS AND OUR COMPREHENSION BECAUSE WE DON'T KNOW WHAT THAT WILL BRING ON US.

Welch David Zuckerberg

"Hmm? My father never told me about this box." That's what the grandma said when Rebecca told her about the box. "Ok... but I prefer to follow his will because he had a strong hunch."

"Alright, Grandma, but I will wear the good luck mace around my neck; after all, you promised me that anything I find in the basement belongs to me! Right?"

"Yes sweetheart I did promise you that, but please be careful." The grandmother told her that with a smile.

A few days passed in peace, Rebecca continued wearing her lucky mace, and by night time she put it on a small table next to her bed when she slept.

The mace started to bring out a very dim light at the same time Captain Brown's ship was entering the Earth's atmosphere.

Chapter Five

Captain Brown had a rapturous welcome for the great accomplishment he did from the rest of his crew.

They spent two and a half years in space on a mission considered the first of its kind. That's what the many media channels said about Captain Brown's expedition.

On the other side, the scientists at NASA started working on analyzing the samples they collected from the asteroid belt.

The results were great and promising a bright future for the space mines and about the samples they had from B 001. They could not find what the secret of those samples was, just speculation with half-baked theorizes?

They also couldn't find any explanations for the material body that was found on B 001 or for the place that came from it.

All that they could say about the chemical formula was it was made of many metals combined together and polymer.

After they checked it out it didn't cause any dangers. The agency decided to give the material body to HOUSTON MUSEUM OF NATURAL SCIENCE.

NASA planned to transpose the material body on Sunday to avoid the traffic. The coincidence occurred when the truck passed from the front of Zuckerberg's stores.

Rebecca was dressing up to go outside when she put on the luck mace around her neck. In that moment, the transportation truck passed her window, and then the eyes of the bird started brightening with a strong red light and the mace was shining with blue lights.

Rebecca was in the front of the mirror; she was shocked from this surprise. With no hesitation, she turned around and she saw the truck passing by the window.

When the truck drove away from Rebecca's window, both lights started going down.

Rebecca ran to the garage and jumped on her bike riving fast after the truck that had NASA logo on it.

In the beginning of the chase, she almost lost track because some people were crossing the street to the nearby church.

After the street was clear again, she managed to catch up with the truck. She got to a close distance that allowed her to see the truck entering the museum from the back door.

The back door was used for shipping and receiving purposes, so the guards locked the gates to start their jobs inside.

"Hello, I see you brought new exhibits," Rebecca said to the guard with a smile.

"Yeah, looks like NASA sent us some new stuff for the museum but I don't know what it is exactly."

"Do you know if they will open it for visitors or will it be stored?"

"Honestly I really don't know ma'am, my duty is to guard the gate and I don't have the answer for your question."

"I have the answer if you are really interested," a voice came from behind.

Rebecca was surprised and turned around to see a handsome guy who looked so manly and intelligent, equipped with a charmed, confident smile.

"Captain Jacob Brown at your service, Ms. Their eyes contacted for a moment, but she didn't know why she felt attracted to him.

Rebecca stopped and said with an obvious confusion: "Sorry for my intrusion, sir, I don't know why I was so taken by this truck!"

Before she got off her bike, she hid her mace inside the leather jacket. Now when she took off the helmet, her jacket was covered with golden waves from her shiny blond hair. Captain Brown was standing his ground completely taken by her beauty looking at her with a smile.

"Rebecca Z. Welch, I forgot to introduce myself, sir, you must know the stories of the great Welch; he is my grandfather and I'm managing the store with my grandma."

"Oh, who doesn't know that great museum? I visit it many times and I loved the place, it's been three years since last visit for me."

"THREE YEARS? Huh, what a studious customer you are!" Rebecca joked.

"Honestly, I've visited your store before my last journey and I'm back for awhile now? I was gone for awhile ago?

"Hey my friend, what kind journey for three years is that? Are you a nautical captain? Or Airplane Capitan?

Captain Brown answered with a wide smile on his face: "None of those, Ms."

Rebecca pulled her lips together feeling strange, then she smiled and said softly: "It doesn't matter, if you are this cute and gentle, you be whatever you want to be. I would love to see you visiting our stores again Captain Brown the next chance. By that I don't mean the next three years!"

"Sure thing, I will see it in the next change I get.

"Alright then, I'll go now, bye."

She walked to her bike, started it up, and headed back home, forgetting totally why she came here in first place.

Damn it, why didn't I ask him about his job's nature? Or what was the cargo of that truck? Is it going to be displayed for visitors or just stocked? I'm a real moron!

Rebecca kept thinking of those questions for the next four days, blaming herself for being dumb.

Then all her answers came out on TV through CHANNEL 7 forecast with the next announcement:

"The museum of natural science in Houston is having a big celebration next Monday. The museum is displaying a very important object with big scientific value.

"It's the unidentified space material body that was found on the asteroid belt zone. Thanks to the agency of NASA that presents the object with other artifacts from outer space to the museum. The museum's management allocated a new suite for the new exhibits; the suite will be opened by Captain Jacob Brown, the leader of the expedition to the asteroid belt."

"WOW he's an astronaut then! He, he, a pilot or nautical captain Rebecca repeated with herself and she attempted to go for the new opening.

Chapter Six

The museum was crowded with people in addition to all the news reporters from many media channels.

There was a big platform in the middle of the hall. Outside the museum, the traffic in the streets was heavy and the police were standing their feet to organize the cars' movement.

Then the glorious NASA Parade with the expedition crew arrived at the red carpet entrance. Then the doors opened for the people to get inside to start the ceremony.

Inside the hall, the museum manager started his speech welcoming the guests and the crew members. Then he started speaking about the expedition and how important it was.

He also talked about the strategic targets of this journey; he praised the crew for what they had accomplished on their journey. The speech now turned to Captain Brown who welcomed the guests and thanked NASA for their trust in him.

He also thanked the museum for creating the new suite. Then he started talking about the expedition and the challenges they faced through it, how they faced each one of these challenges and how they crossed over them.

When Captain Brown started talking about the strange material body, one of the reporters asked Captain Brown about the source of the material body.

"We don't know the source or where it came from, and we have many questions about this object, to be honest with you my friends. The asteroid belt is like pile of puzzles for us. Many Planetary astronomers (also called planetary scientists) focus on the growth, evolution, and death of planets. ... According to the University College London, planetary science "is a cross-discipline field including aspects of astronomy, atmospheric science, geology, space physics, biology and chemistry."

The scientists put a lot of theories based on scientific constants about that spot from the universe but they didn't go far about what happened there. By the way, one of the scientists who had a theory about the Asteroid belt was my grandfather Dr. Brown Wheeler, but he didn't have enough evidence to prove his theory."

So Captain Brown gave a summary about Dr. Wheeler's theory and the missing clue to complete it.

Rebecca kept her eyes moving between Captain Brown and the material body; every time she landed her sight on him, she got more attracted to the way he talked and explained everything.

This time she left her mace inside her handbag and didn't wear it.

When the material body was displayed for the visitors, the media cameras started flashing from everywhere. The material body was surrounded by a circle line made of ropes.

Everybody was taken by the material body with all its secrets surrounding the truth about it. After this, visitors moved to check the rest of the suite.

When Rebecca tried to get closer to the material body, she noticed a low brightening glow up on the top section of the material body. So she figured out there was a connection between the mace of good luck and the material body.

That conclusion hit her with a frightening surprise so she went back home without even noticing how she got there.

Rebecca insisted to know what the connection between these two things was. She kept coming to the museum in hope of getting a chance to get close to the material body.

The crowded visitors kept her away many times with no chance getting of close.

Till one day... A good chance came when a storm covered the city sky resulting in few visitors only that day. Rebecca waited until the hall was empty, almost at the end of the opening hours.

She got close to the material body, and the screen started flashing with blue light. At the same time the red light from the bird's eyes started going up too.

Now she stood in the front of the material body. Suddenly, a small hole opened from the right side of the screen so Rebecca entered the mace in.

The mace landed inside slowly. The bird eyes stopped glowing and stayed on the same level of brightening while the blue screen's light level increased.

Rebecca had a thought to turn the mace inside the material body forward like a key. When she did that, a red loading line started loading on screen slowly.

When the loading line reached half way, the material body started shaking strongly then it started floating from ground.

Rebecca was watching all that was happening around her, but when the material body left the ground, she got scared and screamed: OH MY GOD IT FLIES NOW?!?!

Turning the mace backward and pulling it out of the material body, she ran outside without seeing the screen of the device causing a light that couldn't be seen from the screen.

Rebecca didn't know the Immensity of the disaster she brought on Earth by what she did.

Chapter Seven

Place: Planet AZMEER or the planet of the Black Demons as they call themselves. The planet is located in the ANDRUEMIDA galaxy behind the big dark nebula. It's far from Earth at about 2.5 million light-years away. The guard was on his regular shift which was at an end in the great cosmic observatory struggling with the obvious sleepiness on his face.

When the signal started coming from the "positron sensor" device, he thought he was sleeping at the beginning, until the signal became stronger.

Then he completely woke up and the blood started running in his face. "This can't be... It's impossible... that's it... that's it... I must tell MAD FURY, "he was screaming passionately.

He ran to the headquarters to look for Mad Fury there, at the door of the meeting room. He asked curiously: "Where is Mad Fury?"

"He is in a meeting with the commander and I don't know when it will end," the guard answered.

"Heh, I know when, just give him this paper to see for yourself."

"Okay, sir."

The guard entered the meeting room; on the head of the meeting table was the leader of the 7th fleet, the only force on planet Azmeer.

They were an influential force to be reckoned with and they had a golden age in the power and domination. They possessed a terrible weapon in the past that brought a lot of planets to their knees just by hearing about it. However, they lost that weapon and with it they lost their prestige among the planets.

The session's atmosphere prevailed with stress because the commander received a report about break-ins through the galaxy zone that under the treaty of cosmic peacekeeping. What made the commander even angrier was the guy behind these break-ins was Mad Fury himself.

"For how long will we bear your foolish actions Mad Fury? We don't deny the honorable history of your family in our war. The history that goes for millions of years, we also don't forget you are the carrier of the BLACK SUN SHIELD that you inherited from your ancestors. We were masters of glory in the whole universe, and that glory is gone now with our power and prestige as you know."

"I got to find the forbidden area," Mad Fury said.

"THAT'S ENOUGH!" the commander screamed. "You must stop your insanity, Mad Fury, the situation cannot take any more than this! With your feverish search for the forbidden area, you inspire terror in their hearts. Don't forget they made the peacekeeping treaty to protect themselves from us and that's why they are holding up to it. So when you try to break it you are scaring them and that puts us in danger!"

"They were our slaves! They wouldn't even dare to raise their sights in our faces, now they issued conditions on us? Hehehe."

"You said it yourself, they were, now listen to me, for the last time, and I'm warning you to stop these illusions. I sent my report to the general counsel with a promise it will be the last break-in from our side. Your struggle is useless, Mad Fury; everything we know about that terrible weapon was gone millions of years ago. Our ancestors made sure no one can reach it and use it again."

"Heh, don't mix the facts sir; you know very well the weapon was lost by a plot from the queen."

"I know that, but right now we are living under new terms, so stop causing troubles for something hopeless," the commander told him quietly.

With these words the session was over after Mad Fury was forced to promise he would stop breaking-in the zone for search.

Chapter Eight

"Sir, they sent this paper for you from the observatory. The soldier told Mad Fury after he was done talking with the commander."

"I have a feeling things will change in a big way," Mad Fury was talking to himself when he was heading to the observatory.

It was after midnight, and nobody was left in the building but Carmen. He was waiting for the end of his shift and for Mad Fury after he sent the paper for him.

"Are you sure about the signal, Carmen?" Mad Fury asked trying to cover his emotion.

"Yes, sir, it is still at same level, it has not changed," Carmen said.

"Do you know what the source of the signal is?"

"The black hole's heart, sir."

"Damn it! Do you know how long I dreamed about this? Carmen?"

"Yes, sir, I know."

"Where is the location of the signal?"

"You wouldn't believe where hahaha, close to the remains of planet Cateen, sir."

"WHAT?" Mad Fury screamed. "I searched everywhere in the universe and I put a big reward for all trackers and pirates but nobody found anything! I never thought it would be there."

"Okay, sir, after the dream came true, what are you going to do now?"

"Huh? Oh yes, we need to move as fast as we can," Mad Fury answered while the ideas were running in his head.

"Carmen, do you think any other planets around will notice the signal?"

"Yes, sir, because they have observatories and the same equipment we have; don't forget how much they are afraid we find the black hole's heart."

"Yes, yes, listen Carmen; I need you to do me a favor."

"At your service, sir."

"I want you to change the setting of the sensor now, so it stays working normally without showing the signal."

Carmen removed the cover of the machine from the bottom and started messing with the wires until the signal disappeared.

Then he returned to his chair smiling mischievously. "Hehehe, no one will know about this, only me and you Mad Fury."

"No pal, just me!" Mad Fury said and attacked Carmen from behind.

Chapter Nine

"What just happened? This is just the morning!" the adjutant general said.

"Sir, we found the guard of the observatory killed," the soldier reported through the communicator.

"This is not related to my section, contact the investigation department."

"Sir, there is something fishy going around and I want you to go now to the investigation's office."

"HEY! Is this an order? Don't forget who you are talking to!"

"Yes, sir, it's an order, from the general counsel himself!"

"RIGHT AWAY!" He jumped out of his bed, and within minutes he was standing at the crime scene.

"What happened here?" the general asked.

"Sir, Carmen was found dead when the next guard came to change shifts with him this morning."

"What else? Any trace for the murderer?"

"We don't know exactly, but it could be Mad Fury, one of our soldiers testifies he delivered a note for him from Carmen after yesterday's meeting. After that Mad Fury went to the observatory."

"Mad Fury, I'm completely not comfortable."

"Sir, the counselor wants you at the investigation's office."

The counselor was so angry when he saw the commander and he screamed "WELCOME SLEEPING COMMANDER! WHERE HAVE YOU BEEN, You idiot!?"

The commander was scared and said: "What happened?"

"One of our Space-Time Ship is missing," the investigation's director said.

"NO! This is unbelievable, what about the locator inside the ship?"

"Not working, take this one too, we found another ship in the woods close to the ship's base and it's one of the ships we have wanted on our list."

"Whom does it belong to?"

"The SILENT GHOSTS GANG".

"NO! THIS IS TOO MUCH!" the commander shouted.

"Prepare yourself for a trial," the counsel said.

"Yes, sir."

"Sir counsel, may I have a word?" the investigation's director asked.

"Sure, go ahead."

"I think the commander didn't have a hand in what happened."

"And how is that?"

"You gave Mad Fury more than his capacity with a lot of districts, I bet you he has connections with the SILENT GHOSTS GANG Because if not, how in the hell do you explain their presence in the headquarters at a late hour at night time? And how did they get inside? I'm sure they are on board with Mad Fury on the same ship now, this is all Mad Fury's plan and the commander doesn't have any hand in this. What's really important now is why Mad Fury did all this? Where did he go? What is he planning next? What is he covering by killing Carmen? He just disperses without a clue about his location or the reasons behind all that."

"I will put the commander case on hold for now; do your best to find them." That was last thing the counsel said before leaving.

Chapter Ten

The DOWRBAN or the planet-galaxy as they call it, became an important trade and management center in the chain of Andromeda.

In fact, it was small planet, but what gave it all this significance was the success in deflecting all attacks from planet Azmeer and forcing them to sign the cosmic peacekeeping treaty.

It also contained the headquarters of the GALAXY KNIGHTS a place for the top warriors with high level of fighting skills. They received the perfect training, accepting professionals with no race or sex type required.

In the morning Tai Onatem V was sitting down watching the monitoring screens while he was having his drink. One of the headquarter employees came in and told him about something that he needed to see in person, so he felt uncomfortable.

"What is that?" Tai Onatem asked.

"We got a message on the X positron sensor; there is a signal that came from a very far distance that confirmed a positron activity, probably it's the BLACK HOLE'S HEART.

"DAMN IT! How did you know if it was the black hole's heart?" Tai Onatem asked with temper.

"We analyzed the signal and it's not for a full positron activity, it was a tracking signal."

"This is so bad."

"You didn't hear the worst yet, sir."

"Capitan Palee, what's worse?"

"Any news from Azmeer has never been good, sir."

"WHAT HAPPENED THERE?"

"Our friends there told us that Mad Fury went on the run from justice to an unknown destination after he was accused of killing one of the observatory's guards."

"They also told us that he escaped on a space-time ship and they believe he's on that ship with the Silent Ghosts Gang."

"Dead guard? Space-time ship? Silent ghosts? Mad Fury, unknown destination? Signal from the black hole heart? It's a full menu!"

"How long has this signal been emitting?"

"Ten hours so far, sir."

"Captain Palee, yellow alert-level C, immediate meeting for all the knights with no excuses for any reasons, NOW!"

"Roger that, sir."

The meeting hall was crowded with knights, and everybody was whispering about the reasons for this meeting and the alert.

Tai Onatem came in with Captain Palee, and speedily walked to the platform. There was Yo-Zuri with them, and so everybody got quiet especially when they saw Yo-Zuri coming in.

They called for Yo-Zuri. *There must be something very dangerous happening*, they thought. Some of the knights were whispering.

Tai start the meeting: "I call for you today for a serious and dangerous matter, some of you may have heard about Mad Fury and what's going on now because him. What we are facing now is threatening our existence. Our planet and all other planets are in big danger if our fears come true. We lived through dark ages because the Azmeerians infuriated and they lost all their power after the loss of their main weapon. After that, all that was left for them was Mad Fury's insane searches for their lost glory. I don't deny some of you think all that was just stories from millions of years ago. But what happened today proved all these stories are real. First, we received a signal from the positron sensor for a weak positron activity; we think it belongs to the black hole's heart." The crowed start whispering.

"Second, we know from our resources that Mad Fury flew after the signal with some of the Silent Ghosts Gang. What really matters are, do you know where the signal comes from? It came from the solar system that once had the planet Cateen, which was totally destroyed in a single day. After a quick study of planet Earth I chose my team members who will join me.

"Yo-Zuri will be the first knight. Also I will take with me ROCK, RAIN, and WINDY. I know about their abilities on controlling the forces of nature. After preparing the team with all necessary equipment, we will leave to planet Earth as soon as we can. We don't know what we will face there, but it's better to be ready for anything that might happen there... may the gods be with us."

Chapter Eleven

"We are entering the airspace of the planet Earth, sir."

"Hold on a little, I want a report about the nature of this planet and the advances of the human race," Mad fury said.

"There are a lot of electromagnetic waves loaded with digital information."

"Okay, copy all this information beside the languages of the planet and upload it to the brain feeding device so we can understand all these languages."

After five hours, the team of death was ready.

"Now go on the way of the black hole's heart and get it. I want a real terror on this planet, show MERCY TO NO ONE!"

It was so dark when the ghosts drowned forward to the museum united in the darkness of the night; in just seconds they were next to the museum.

"FINALLY! We are here, the first to see this weapon after millions of years!"

"You don't know how powerful this weapon is; we have to move fast and complete our job. We have to find the FORBIDDEN ZONE that carries the great arsenal."

"With all the weapons that are in there, We will regain control of the whole universe

"How we can locate the forbidden zone?"

"We have to complete charging the launch sequence so the black hole's heart travels to the forbidden zone."

"How are we supposed to do that, Fury?"

"We must find the control key; this operation is not easy at all."

"I CAN DESTROY THIS PLANET ALL BY MY SELF TO GET WHAT I WANT!" Laiosh said.

"HEH and then how can we find the key smart Laiosh? If the person who holds the key is killed by mistake, all our effort and waiting will be gone for good."

"DAMN IT! What's the solution then?"

"Leave this to me!" Mad Fury said.

Mad Fury moved toward the black hole's heart and put his hand on it.

This move made the entire building shake very hard, then Mad Fury started shooting neutron lasers from his weapon at different directions which caused a large damage to the building.

"Now they will know we came for the device. I will leave this small robot so I can see who will get close to the black hole's heart."

Mad Fury set a small and highly advanced robot and hid it in one of the corners in the building to closely watch everyone who gets near the black hole's heart.

"Let's get back to our ship now; those humans need to know we were here, FIRE THE NEUTRON CANONS AROUND THE BUILDING!"

"Why don't we threaten them directly, Fury and demand what we want from them?"

"HEH, you will know why later, my friends."

The ship of the gang flew around the place making Immense damage

and causing a real terror. The emergency troops had been alerted with the rest of government's security departments to control the situation.

Captain Brown was called to come in the operations center and there the officer in charge met him.

"Captain Brown, I'm sorry we had to call you to come here that fast, but it's a serious matter and we need your experience."

"This is the first time we face a direct attack from aliens. The evidence also shown that material body you brought with you from space is what got them here; we need to move fast."

Captain Brown headed to the museum with the emergency team and he wasn't surprised when he saw the destruction because he felt what was coming was even worse. When they reached the black hole's heart, they found it vibrating very powerfully.

"It wasn't like this last time we saw it, what happened?" Captain Brown was wondering.

"I don't know, sir."

Brown turned around his head in the place searching and looking closely. After a while he asked the team commander, "Can I see the surveillance cameras?"

"Of course, only if they are still working."

The team ran to the cameras room in the museum and they started playing back the video tapes to the time the ship arrived.

They saw how Fury put his hand on the device and how it was vibrating and then he started shooting with his gun around.

"It looks like the material body is what made them come to our planet, gentlemen. Let us leave from here now; we are facing a non-easy enemy that we need to prepare to face.

Brown was thinking deeply when the soldiers started moving, so he stopped them by saying, "WAIT! This material body was in space for millions of years, then I brought it here many months ago. So all that time they didn't notice it! What happened now? There must be something that activated the material body. I want to stay here and check all the videos since the day we brought the object here to the day of the aliens' appearance."

Brown stayed alone in the monitoring room watching every single video hoping to find any evidence until he got to the day before the attack on the museum.

Specifically, the thunder storm's day, he was following the screen with tired eyes till suddenly he opened his eyes widely and said with a feeding voice: "REBECCA!"

Chapter Twelve

The phone rang at Zuckerberg stores, and Rebecca answered:

"Hello, how can I help you?"

"Rebecca Welch Zuckerberg! WHAT DID YOU DO ARE YOU CRAZY?" The person on the phone was screaming!

Rebecca, scared, asked: "Who the hell are you?"

Captain Brown calmed himself down then he spoke quietly: "We are in a serious situation and I believe the threat we face is because of... YOU! Please, I need you to come to the museum immediately."

The sun was about to go down when Rebecca rode her bike toward the museum. Brown was waiting for her at the gate.

When she walked to him she was afraid and shaking. He grabbed her arm and took her to the space material body and he said to her: "SPEAK!"

She told him with details all that happened to her, starting with the box she found in the basement to the minute of activating the black hole's heart.

All this time they didn't see Mad Fury's robot that was teleporting the sound and pictures very clear.

"So where is this mace now?"

"It's in my house. When you called me I came in hurry so I forgot it there."

"Let's go home and get it."

They drive Rebecca's bike, and Fury's robot was flying after them.

When they got inside the store, Rebecca brought the wooden box. Brown was surprised with what the box contained.

Then he saw the old other half of the missing manuscript that his grandpa told him about.

"OH MY GOD! All these years it was here! And my poor old man spent his life searching for it? And nobody believed my grandpa? DAMN IT, DAMN IT!"

"Don't worry about the manuscript, it's yours, but now let us find a way out of this problem now." That's what Rebecca said to Brown.

"Let's take your mace and go back to the museum," Brown told Rebecca with a tided voice after he hid the manuscript in Chest pocket.

Thoughts were running madly in Brown's head: *What should I do now? We reached a critical stage!* He was thinking without noticing the robot behind them.

When they reached the black hole's heart, he grabbed the mace and move towards it slowly.

A few steps away from it and… suddenly, a strong voice came from up above!

"STOP RIGHT THERE! YOUR LINE ENDS HERE!"

That was Mad Fury flying and he landed on ground with his silent ghosts who were covered all in black.

"Who are you? And what do you want from us?" Brown asked.

"My name is Mad Fury; I know you will never forget this name ever! I came from planet Azmeer to restore what my people have lost millions years ago, NOW GIVE ME THE KEY IN YOUR HAND AND SAVE YOUR LIFE!"

"No, not before I know what this material body is, what does it mean to you? And how should I grantee the safety of the people of Earth from you?"

Here Mad Fury shouts: "ENOUGH! I GAVE YOU MORE THAN YOUR TIME YOU LOW-GRADE CREATURE! NOW YOU ALL WILL SEE WHO MAAAD FURRRYYYY IS!"

In that moment, a group of soldiers surrounded the area and told everybody to surrender immediately.

Mad Fury and his gang didn't give them a second; they started shooting neutrons from their weapons and the results were horrible. As soon as the neutrons touched their bodies, they disappeared!

The next target for Fury was Rebecca and Capitan Brown. Rebecca closed her eyes and surrendered to her fate.

She was surprised that the shots didn't reach them!

Out of nowhere they were covered with a clear shield from every side!

Mad Fury and his ghosts went crazy when they saw this. Mad Fury screamed: "WHAT'S THIS? WHO'S THERE?"

"WE ARE HERE, FURY! AND I'M SENDING YOU TO HELL! THIS TIME I PROMISE YOU, YOU WONT GET AWAY FROM MY HAAAAAAND!"

"HAHAHAHA! Tai Onatem V! You really think you can defeat us all by yourself?? I'm sure you lost your mind!"

"We are not going to leave all the fun for Tai only, FURY!" Windy said that and she was with Rock and Rain.

"You will never be able to defeat us! There is no hope!" Fury said.

Suddenly, they were surrounded by lightning from every side, and then a stormy strong voice came from nowhere: "NO! YOU ARE THE ONE WHO HAS NO HOPE WITH US!"

They were thrown strongly through the wall to the outside of the museum by the thunder.

Then Yo-Zuri appeared with the armor of the gray thunder that was covering all his body except his face.

The entry of Yo-Zuri to the battlefield really scared them because everybody knew his bravery and his power too; they also called him GOD OF THUNDER.

"Laiosh, Amrash, Koru—SHOW THEM THE POWER OF THE SILENT GHOSTS!" Mad Fury screamed.

"With our pleasure, sir!"

The three ghosts combined together and took the shape of a giant existence, dark and gloomy; it was shining with red flame from the eyes and mouth.

The giant monster attacked Yo-Zuri who stepped in with a powerful strike from his famous weapon "Thunder's chain", and sliced the monster in two pieces.

Now the situation became even more difficult; they became two monsters now but they had the same size and same power!

They attacked Yo-Zuri from front and behind at the same time with their spears. Yo-Zuri deflected their attack and countered back with his weapon, shattering them in four monsters now.

"STOP Yo-Zuri! We will not defeat them this way!" Tai said to him.

Tai called for the others: "Let's go guys! Show them some of what we have! Come with me Rain, you too Windy!"

Rain had the ability to control the element of water, and Windy could control the force of air and wind. Rock had control on the element of soil and stones.

The three knights worked together and created a huge wall from water and rocks while the winds were blowing on top of the wall. The wall stood between Yo-Zuri and the evil ghosts.

Fury interrupted using the black sun's armor and destroyed the giant wall while the ghosts carried on attacking, taking the shape of dark monsters even bigger than the first one!

"I have to use my special power or we are doomed!" Tai was talking to himself.

Tai had a many special abilities and one of those abilities was rising up the concentrating power of the mind for any knight in the field.

So he asked Rain and Windy to grab his hands standing between them and said: "Now focus your power together to create a giant of water and winds. Yo-Zuri will support the giant with lightning." They follow Tai's instructions and it was a real big giant lightning with thunder!

"NOW! IT'S YOUR TURN ROCK, SUMMON THE GIANT OF FLAMING LAVA! Yo-Zuri, ATTACK WITH YOUR THUNDER!"

Tai screamed, "NOW MULTIPLY!" Now there were two water giants with another two giants made from rocks and flaming lava, and they all attacked at once.

The flame giants where shooting fire rocks like hell, while the water giants hit the dark ghosts with thunder water!

The Ghost Gang Giants couldn't hold much longer so they were pushed back by the attack.

"DAMN IT; we must show them our true power!" Fury shouted and attacked with his neutron weapon. He attacked one of the rock giants, and with one hit, he cut the giant's leg and this caused the giant to crumble to the ground.

Then one of the dark beasts grabbed the water giant and threw it on the wounded rocky giant. They both exploded with white lightning and disappeared.

"HAHAHAHA, YOU WILL NEVER DEFEAT ME Tai!" Fury screamed.

"You stupid fool! I will use every single stone and drop of water on this planet to fight you! You will never hold up, I will make hundreds of these giants, YOU WILL SEEEE!"

"Sir, they found the weak point of our giants, what we should do now?"

"Heh, don't worry; our weak point will be our victory's weapon!" Tai told them with confidence.

"How is that, sir?"

"Just do as I say."

Tai's plan was creating four more giants, two water and two rocks, so the total was six strong giants.

The powerful creatures now surrounded the Ghost Gang Giants from all sides; they were spinning around them shooting their weapons at them so the ghosts were trapped in a locked circle. Now the giants locked them up with no way to escape!

The giants started crushing on each other putting the ghosts in the middle, and the giants of water were crushing on rock's giant.

"NOW Yo-Zuri! IT'S YOUR TURN!" Tai said.

Yo-Zuri releases huge circles of thunder around both the giants and the ghosts and… BOOOOOMM! It was a massive explosion that took away the ghosts and the giants and they disappeared from the face of Earth!

Chapter Thirteen

Cries of victory were heard everywhere from the knights and people of Earth who were watching the great battle on screens.

"We owe you our lives as long as we live my brave knights!" The commander of the emergency troops said, welcoming the heroes at the operations center. Rebecca and Brown were there too.

"This is our duty, sir; we have devoted ourselves to fight evil everywhere," Tai replied.

"God thanks you comrades! Now, can you tell us the whole story about everything that happened? All people of Earth want to know how things were started."

"Alright then, I will start from beginning. The story begins millions years ago when there was that small planet between planets Jupiter and Mars. The planet's name was "Cateen"; it was one of the most famous centers of science in the whole universe. And because the peaceful and politic nature of people on planet Cateen, they lived in peace, they never had a war. They reached very advanced levels of academic sciences. Even the other planets used to send their scientists to planet Cateen for study and development.

"Things stayed the same way until one day, a scientist came from plant Azmeer to study the positron controlling science. The positron is known as the ANTI-MATTER ENERGY. A scientist named Merdad told them he wanted to make a device that could resist the effect of the black hole on space ships traveling between planets.

"But the real purpose of Merdad's visit was absolutely different. He was sent by the governor of Azmeer to study that part of science so he could create a terrible weapon that served the ambitions and the sick dreams of Sattola the governor of planet Azmeer!

"Merdad stayed for a long time in planet Cateen for study. One day, Sattola visited planet Cateen and he met princes Elena He really liked the princess and she liked him too. A while after that, they were married

so she went back with him to planet Azmeer and she became the queen.

"Merdad returned to Azmeer and started to work on the weapon. After some time he started working on the final steps of designing the "Forbidden zone" The forbidden zone is a giant space station. The purpose of it was to make containers for ANTI-MATTER ENERGY with different sizes.

"He was working without stop to put the forbidden zone to work. All that was with minimum numbers of employees to keep it a secret until It was completed with a personal observation by Sattola himself. The idea of this weapon is to make a containers filled with the positron, then release it through the holes of container and control it by a magnetic field according to very accurate scientific calculations.

"The result would be really terrible! When it started working, a single container could create a black hole that had the ability to envelope a whole planet and destroy it totally! They named the container the Black Hole's Heart. It's the same one that gave the signal and brought Mad Fury to the Earth.

"The first victim was planet "Jorana" One of the most mortal enemies of the Azmeerians; Sattola gave them a few days to surrender or face death. The people of that planet didn't accept to surrender so Sattola, sent only one ship to them. When they saw the lonely ship they start laughing… but the result was indescribable! The ship releases two containers on the sides of the poor planet. The planet fell between two black holes turning it to small pieces in a few hours only! No one and nothing survived from the black holes… not even the dust of the planet!

"Many planets submitted to Sattola. Those who resisted or went against him faced the same fate as the planet Jorana. In just two years, ten planets were wiped out from existence. The names of Sattola and Azmeer became the most frightening names in our galaxy. Day after day, Sattola became real sadistic and he didn't stop what he was doing, so he gave his order to make a special armor for him to wear in his battles.

"Merdad created the black sun's armor; it was a terrifying armor. Anyone who wore it gained the control of anti-matter energy. In every battle, he had the first strike and kept fighting, killing, till he was head to toes covered with blood. After that, he set off the black hole's heart to destroy what's left from his poor victims.

"As his power was growing, the number of Sattola's enemies grew even bigger, then he ordered Merdad again to make a special key. The person who had this key could enter the warfare arsenal in the forbidden zone. Anyone else who got close to this area without the key was destroyed automatically.

"For more protection, he surrounded the forbidden zone with a field of the anti-matter energy and he hid it in the center of the dark nebula. After a while, Merdad was assassinated by his many enemies. Sattola was sorrowful for lowing Merdad. Felt immense sorrow. He was his right hand and a close friend too.

"Many years have passed and Sattola kept his madness and his plan of bringing the universe under his feet. Day after day, the life on planet Azmeer and everything else became dark, just as if life was fleeing away from the planet. On the other side, the queen kept complaining with some of the close retinue. She was always talking to him: 'What happened to you Sattola? Your heart has become stone! Please, what you're doing is madness, do you know how bad our reputation has become? Our name now is compared with bad things and Epidemics! Where is that nice guy that I fell in love with?'

"'Hahahaha, please honey, forget about this now, you became too sensitive, now we are the masters of the universe!' he replied. But the queen was planning something against him; she planned to steal the key to the forbidden zone along with something else. The black sun's armor had a controlling device on the shape of black sun with red lines of flames coming out of it. Without this part, the armor loses 75 percent of its power!

"'This is the perfect way to stop Sattola's madness!' She was talking to one of her closest attendents. 'But my lady, the consequences will be big; maybe it will cost you your life too?' 'I DON'T CARE! We must sacrifice so the others can survive Sattola's wrath, do you know how many planets were gone? HOW MANY LIVES WERE TAKEN? I can hear them screaming in my ears! It needs to be stopped at any cost!'

"'I'm with you my dear lady, to the last drop of my blood.' The queen smiled with sadness and said: 'Your part in my plan is big, you will be chased for the rest of your life, and you will never come back to your family and the people you love. Death will be easier than this, you will have to disperse, cut your roots. They will be chasing you like rabid hounds with no mercy! That's a very big sacrifice.'

"'My lady, if that will stop bloodshed... I will accept gladly!' 'Your bravery is rare! You are a true knight, Tie.' That was Tai Onatem the first Galaxy Knight. Sattola used to put those two pieces next to his bed when he's sleeping because he didn't feel safe to put them anywhere else, with heavy guards on them. One night, the queen entered his room and took the two pieces quietly and that happened during Tai's shift.

"When the king woke up in the morning, first thing he turned his sight to was the two pieces and... THEY WERE NOT THERE! Sattola went mad and with a devilish voice he screamed: 'GUUUAAAAAARRRDDSS!' In a second, all the guards summoned in front of him: 'YES SIR!'

FOOLS! WHERE ARE The key to the forbidden zone and the control to my armor!? THEY WERE HERE LAST NIGHT! WHO ENTER MY ROOM? GET ME EVERYBODY RIGHT HERE, RIGHT NOW! SHUT DOWN ALL GATES AND AIRPORTS! NO TRAVELING BY ANY SHIP FOR ANY DISTANCE! MOOOVEEE IT!'

"He was screaming like a maniac, grabbed his sword and ran out his room to the queen's room. He found her sitting peacefully, staring out the window. 'Do you know what happened, Elena? Someone broke into my room and stole my control key and t...' 'It was me, Sattola!' She said that with very quiet voice... the room floated with silence for few seconds...

"Then he attacked her at once grabbing her beautiful face and shouted, 'HOW DARE YOU!' With a single hit he sent her to the ground. 'WHERE ARE THEY NOW? START TALKING, I SAID!' He put his sword on her throat but she said with pain, 'Ahh... you... will never... find th... e... m!' Sattola gave away the sword and stood her up on her feet, pushed the poor queen to the wall and continued: 'TALK NOW AND TALK FAST! WHERE ARE MY THINGS?'

"'Tai took them away and ran in a space-time ship! You will never ever find him, Sattola! Now Sattola knew what dilemma he fell in; these two pieces couldn't be re-made, especially after Merdad's death. And what made things even worse was that those pieces didn't send tracking signals unless someone tried to mess them up, or destroy them!

"Oh… one more thing! Let us not forget the options of traveling in time and places by the space-time ship! It has the ability and flexibility to travel freely between the time and space. That made finding Tai Onatem impossible. With all these thoughts in his head, Sattola felt the situation he was facing was closing up on him so tight! The crazy king stared at the face of his ex-beloved queen for a while… then he started talking very low.

"'I promise you will regret what you've done… you won't imagine the torture that you will receive… that… I promise you… my dear!' Sattola gave his straight order to the soldiers to start searching for Tai anyway; he knew that Tai would not try to break the pieces or mess them up. He also tried to enter the forbidden zone, of course with all the defense systems around it and with no key that was impossible.

"With the days running away, the hope in retrieving the stolen objects started to fade away. Sattola grew nerves and violent. He did not forget about the queen so he ordered her to be in a lonely single jail and give her a rough treatment. One night he visited her in the cell and he was standing behind the glass, watching her. Then he entered to find her sitting in peace without paying attention to her misery.

"'So… how do you see the life of prison? Is it better than the life of the throne and the high class lifestyle?' 'No darling, a peaceful mind is a lot better than all that!' She walked toward him with her eyes shining with victory and she said to him: 'You have no idea how deeply I sleep now that I guaranteed your butchering is over and my conscience is not torturing me anymore'.

"Sattola started thinking evilly; the last words the queen said gave him an idea about how to get his revenge from the queen! 'Peaceful conscience you said? And what is your CONSCIENCE going to feel if you knew you will be the reason for a new massacre for the closest people to your heart?' 'WHAT ARE YOU GOING TO DO? YOU MONSTER!' 'HAHAHA, you will see for yourself... yes, you WILL SEE!'

"Sattola started preparing his revenge plan against the queen. He was holding one last container fully loaded. Putting both on one ship, Sattola took the last container and the queen with him heading to planet Cateen. The queen was tied to a chair when Sattola put her at the big window in the ship to face her planet... for the last time! 'What would be your feeling if you knew that the destruction of your planet with all your people is because of you? And you will see all that with your own eyes.'

"'So be it!' Sattola released the black hole's heart on the poor planet Cateen while Elena watched the destruction of her homeland, while her eyes filled with tears! Elena returned to her cell, crying for many months and could not take the painful images out of her head, till her face became pale like the dead. After this, Sattola decided to execute the queen at the public hall.

"The hall was full with people; they came to say goodbye to the nice queen. There came the sweet Elena in a wagon without even cover. She was saying 'goodbye' to the crowd with her sad eyes and then she became quiet with a weird look. 'Now it's time!' The executioner got close to her and pointed to her with the sword to put her neck on the edge. She kneeled and closed her eyes, and then in just a second ... the sword landed on her beautiful neck!

"All the crowd was asking quietly: 'Where is Sattola? Why has nobody seen him?'"

Rebecca said: "Oh, the poor guy, he couldn't stand the execution."

"Hahahaha, he was there, but nobody saw him!"

"Is this a puzzle, Tai? How was he there but no one saw him?" Brown asked Tai.

"He was the executioner!" There was a moment of silence.

"TERRIBLE! He is a criminal and a real maniac…"

"Indeed he was. He stayed like this till one day they found him dead in his room but we don't know if someone killed him or he just killed himself. After all these events, the power shift turned around in the galaxy and Azmeer signed the treaty of peacekeeping. But there are still some of the Azmeerians who dream of the return of their lost glory, like Fury. In time, people started saying it's a myth that no one needs to worry from, and about us, the Cavalry Regiment we were ready and stood by to face any danger or threat from the return of the "Forbidden Zone". After Sattola's death, the Azmeerians' hope died in retrieving the forbidden zone, while we the knights kept on defending justice and innocent people around the galaxy and the universe throughout the years. So we decided to open a center to recruit the heroes and anyone who wants to apply to our regiment that has the ability to fight evil.

"It appears that Tai first hid the two pieces on planet Earth at a different time from his own. Yes he did use the space-time ship in a clever way! Nobody could predict what happened to him or to planet Cateen."

"No my friend," Brown said, "My grandfather predicted that about planet Cateen. He was sure these asteroids used to be a whole planet that was destroyed by the hands of somebody! My poor grandpa didn't have the evidence to prove that, and today I have the clues from your story… Now he will rest peacefully in his grave

Brown got quiet for half a minute, and then he asked Tai Why Fury didn't use his power to locate the objects.

"I already told you, Brown. These two pieces don't give any tracking signals unless someone turns them on. Now, he knows where to find them."

"OOOHHH MMMYYY GOOOD! GRANDMA! NOOOOO!" Rebecca screamed and she ran outside like crazy!

Brown said to the others: "Let's hurry up and save her! Fury must be on his way to retrieve the other part of his armor!"

"Oh my god! If he will get his hand on that piece he will became invincible!"

They arrived to... what's left of Zuckerberg's stores. Rebecca was standing there like a statue and the tears were running down from her eyes.

Brown put his hand on her shoulder from behind. She turned around and he held her in his arms. Then she cried like a baby.

Rebecca was repeating through her tears: "My grandma... my house! My grandma... MY HOUSE! Everything is gone now, Brown! I killed her! I KILLED MY DEAR SWEET GRANDMA WITH MY OWN HANDS! Now all is lost!"

"No my dear, that wasn't your fault... it wasn't!" Brown said.

"FURY WILL PAY FOR ALL THIS, REBECCA... I PROMISE YOU!" Tai said to her.

Chapter Fourteen

The joy of victory turned to a sadness and sorrow, after the knights defeated the ghosts. Fury shifted the power balance to his side.

Right after he completed the black sun's armor, he gave forty-eight hours for the people of Earth to hand him the key to the forbidden zone.

The defending force of Earth tried to stand in Fury's face. A group of air fighters were trying to shoot him down but... the result of the battle was so fast and beyond all imaginations.

All that he had to do was wave simply with one hand, causing a pure energy in the size of an egg, exploding in silence and starting to grow so fast to cover the fighters with white thunder and they all melted by the power of the radiation and the fighters simply vanished!

Then the same fate was waiting for the atomic carriers.

"What to do now, knights?" Brown asked.

Tai was thinking: *I don't know, the situation is really hard now, fighting or surrendering both means DEATH! guess we have no options my brothers.*

"WE WILL FIGHT TILL DEATH! We are the knights. We do not fear death," Yo-Zuri said.

"Yo-Zuri, it's not important if we died bravely... the dilemma is even bigger than that. If we fight and die, or surrender, Fury will get the key to the forbidden zone anyway and that will lead to the destruction of the whole universe! We must defeat Fury and destroy him at any cost! We have no other options, everybody needs to realize that!" Tai said that tidily.

Brown was thinking deeply for a while, then suddenly his eyes started brightening with a strange light and he said with a steady voice, "I have a hellish plan... I will destroy the forbidden zone!"

He looked in the other people's eyes and they were astonished!

"WHAT? Are you crazy? Did you find it in the first place so you can destroy it? Even if you find it, how are you going to destroy it anyway? I think you need to get some rest, my friend!" Then everybody started giving comments about Brown and laughing.

Brown waited until they were done commenting on what he said. With a confident smile, he start explaining...

"THE PRODIGAL SON'S RETURN, this is the code name for this operation. Tai told us that the black hole's heart is a container that has the anti-matter energy. And by experience we have proven that the key can activate the black hole's heart. So my plan is like this... we will plant a hydrogen bomb inside the black hole's heart and send it back to the forbidden zone. As soon it arrives there it will explode inside the zone and rip it into pieces inside out. Tie told me the black hole's heart top cover will open automatically when it's inside the forbidden zone for reloading."

Tie followed Brown: "Then the key will be of no use... BRILLIANT PLAN BROWN!"

"Fury will be really angry, he could kill us all," Rebecca said.

"He wants to kill us anyway," Yo-Zuri said.

"We will fight with all our powers; let him know we are not easy bait for evil like him. I can't deny that Fury became so powerful with the armor of the black sun... but be sure we will crush his neck."

"What's important now is gaining time for the plan. Deadline is in thirty-six hours from now... I will reply to Fury that we want to fight him at the big desert."

Brown said: "I think two days are enough for our scientists to plant the bomb in the container. We will be two teams; first team will stay here making sure the planting goes right. I will lead the first team by myself and Rebecca will stay with me. Second team under Tai's lead will go to fight Fury. When we are done with the bomb we will join the second team in the fight at great Nevada desert."

Everyone took their place according to Brown's plan.

"I want you to take Fury's attention away. This is very important, our scientists started working on the hydrogen bomb and they will implant it in the "Black Hole's Heart" at the moment Fury shows up in Nevada."

The bomb became ready in a short time. The scientists drove around the museum in armored cars, disguised by commercials and posters, to keep suspicions away.

Now it was the time! Fury showed in Nevada.

Brown and Rebecca jumped out of the truck, and Brown took the control key from her. He inserted the key in the controlling board, then he turned it against the screen's direction.

The container stopped shaking little by little and landed on floor. Brown kept turning the key in same way then the top part slid open!

"It's all yours now, gentlemen! How long will it take to put the bomb in?"

"About ten hours, sir," the scientist's leader says.

"Ok then, attach the detonator on the top cover from inside. The explosion will happen when the cover is opened. Let's pray for Tai and the other knights to stand for ten hours in the face of that demon."

There was a weird silence around the area when Fury arrived there; the soft air was blowing quietly around him.

Then the winds start whispering: "Hi Fury, finally you came, we have been waiting for you too long." Then the winds took shape of a nice looking girl who started walking in front of Fury.

"Hey... Windy, it's you, I didn't think the knights would accept you to be the first victim?"

Fury was planning to enjoy his revenge from the knights; they often stood in his face and his sick dreams. Now he possessed the black sun's armor and very soon the forbidden zone too.

"I will play with them first, and then I will kill them at once." That was his plan for the fight.

Fury didn't attack in the beginning. That was his deadly mistake. Tai rose up the mind ability's power for the higher level in the knights.

This move gave the knights more powers to combine with the Earth's elements and gave them more flexibility in control with their fighting scales.

In a moment, Windy locked up on Fury with a huge whirlwind sucking up the oxygen away from Fury. Fury found himself facing suffocation and couldn't take a single breath.

He started shooting his neutron gun but it was useless, and the Antimatter energy didn't help him too because everywhere he moved, the whirlwind moved with him.

He went down on his knees to the ground... then the ground started shaking lightly under his feet and he lost his balance.

Before he fell again, Fury didn't have the time to reach the ground... BLAAASH! The ground exploded with a strong wave of water!

The water now combined with the wind, and made together a powerful water tornado! The tornado also had rocks in it and started hitting Fury very... very hard!

"NOW ROCK! THE KNOCKOUT! THE DEATH CUBE! Tai screamed.

In a few seconds, Fury was trapped in a big cube made from rocks and he was tied up by ropes made from the titanium; Fury got stuck inside the cube.

Yep, Fury was inside the cube now with all the water and the winds together, and couldn't move as every finger on his hands tied with a rope!

The cube was flying in the air with everything inside... and of course Fury too! Then Yo-Zuri attacked with thunder to finish him off.

Fury was now completely paralyzed with the attack of Yo-Zuri: wind, water, rocks, and thunder, and mighty ropes! Just imagine!

"FINALLY! We've captured this demon alive!" Tie said.

"NO! I WILL KILL HIM BY MYSELF!" Yo-Zuri said.

Yo-Zuri faced the cube and increased the level of the thunder on the cube... this move had a bad effect on the battle line.

The over power caused the power tank on Fury's gun to explode, causing a vertical wave of power shattering the cube and releasing Fury in his last breath!

PHEW! That was too close. Fury went on his knees trying to catch his breaths. Rock attacked with his sword but Fury surrounded himself with the anti-matter energy.

Mad Fury grabbed Rock's hand and it melted right away while poor Rock screamed in severe pain! Then he took Rock's sword and stabbed him deep in the chest while he was smiling in Rock's face!

"Whose turn is it now?" Fury asked with an evil laugh... Windy and Rain attacked with full power! However, the demon Fury stood his ground and all that he did was clapped his hands together causing a wave of pure energy... Rock and Windy were gone with a blink of an eye!

Like a furious tiger, he attacked Yo-Zuri and Tai. Yo-Zuri stood in his face to protect Tai after he covered himself with a pure white shield of thunder.

Fury kept attacking him nonstop, and when the shield started breaking down, Yo-Zuri looked at Tai with tears in his eyes.

"FORGIVE ME MY FRIEND! IT WAS MY FAULT, I DESTROYED US ALL! If you survive… reve… n… ge…to meeee!" Then he took off his favorite weapon, the thunder fists, which was two hand bracelets that went with the thunder shield. These were his last words before he was gone forever.

"Tai Onatem the fifth! And the last one too! HAHAHAHAHA! How would you like to DIE brave knight? Aren't you going to ask? Well, I'm sorry anyway, all that I have on menu is a VERY S… L… O… W, AND PAINFUL DEATH!" The black sun armor started glowing very quietly.

"I will never let you have fun in this, FURY!"

Tai jumped back with a full cover of pure energy and started directing several hits on Fury who replied by absorbing the shots and kept moving forward with confidence.

With one strike, he sent Tie to the ground then he stood on top of him, and then Fury put his hand on Tai's chest and rose up the pressure on Tai!

Tai felt the heat and also felt his chest start ripping apart slowly… Fury said with hatred in his voice: "I JUST WANT YOU TO KNOW… I REALLY ENJOYED THIS!"

His fist shined with strong light and he locked on Tai's face… before he strike him, he felt a strong move and an object launching from somewhere.

"NO! IT'S THE BLACK HOLE'S HEART! YOU FOOLS! WHAT HAVE YOU DONE! SPEAK NOW YOU DAMN… WHAT'S HAPPENING?

"Ye… s, you… are right… it's the black hole's heart… but you need to know it's heading back to the forbidden… zo… ne, haha… ha… ha. It will reach there so fast; you will not catch up with it!

You lost your chance to find the zone Fury… hahaha." Tai was laughing with pain while he was dying.

Fury left Tai and flew to his ship, fired it up and started chasing the speedy black hole's heart and followed it on the computer to locate the forbidden zone.

At the same time, the people in NASA were monitoring and taking the same steps to follow the line of the black hole' heart.

Fury kept chasing the flying object till he entered the area of the dark nebula. The signals kept coming on the radar… suddenly… the black hole's heart disappeared!

"I FOUND IT! FINALLY I FOUND THE FORBIDDEN ZONE!"

He started dreaming about himself entering the zone and retrieving the legendary warfare arsenal that was lost for millions of years, along with the Azmeerians glory!

Suddenly, the cosmic radiations readings increased rapidly.

In a split second… the dark nebula shined with many bright atomic explosions… BAAAAM! BOOOOM! KAAATTAAAABOOOOOMMM!

"NNNNOOOOOOOOOOO!!!!!!!" Fury screamed when he saw the forbidden zone torn apart and turned into dust!

The observers in NASA were following every small reading on their radars. "SIR! The explosion of the targeted area was done perfectly. We spotted a huge wave of the anti-matter energy from the dark nebula. It must have been released from the container in the forbidden zone.

After a while, NASA indicated the birth of a very huge black hole in the same spot of the zone.

Fury's ship was gone from the radars too... "The black hole must have swallowed him, sir."

"Hmmm, we don't know exactly," Brown said.

Chapter Fifteen

"Hey my friend, how are you holding up?" Brown was talking to Tai.

"Haha, as you can see, I don't have much left in me… what's the news?"

"I don't really know," Brown answered. "It's been a while after destroying the forbidden zone with no sign of Fury."

Tai said, "I know my friend, it's not easy to predict what's coming next, but we should be ready. If Fury came back, he will not have mercy on anyone on this planet… believe me!"

"What we should do then?" Browne wondered.

"I'm not going to lie to you; we are in critical condition now, my strongest knights are dead now, and for myself I can barely stand my ground. Even if we call the others for help they will not make it in time. I doubt it if they can even stand in Mad Fury's face! We need a miracle."

Brown put down his head and started thinking as usual.

"Hahaha… what did you find, commander? I start to recognize that look on your face! Have you found a solution?" Tai was joking.

Brown smiled and asked Tai, "Do you think you can read the manuscript that your grandfather Tai Onatem the first wrote down?"

"Sure I can."

"Nice, then let me get it from my car now."

Tie started reading it right away: "Aahhh... I can't understand this, the manuscript is uncompleted and it doesn't have any meaning for what's written. Here you can see graphics by your people about landing zone for space ships beside some symbols back to their time, I don't know but there is a big part missing here."

"Hold on Tai, what you see here is half the manuscript only, I found it in Rebecca's store, but the other part was found by my grandfather! He found it in one of his expeditions. He built his theory on it but nobody believed him for he was short on evidence. He was missing this part you have in your hands now, what an ironic fate! He died before he knew he was right."

"Where is the other part now Brown?"

"It's in my house... I will go and get it now." Then he left.

Brown drove his car to the house he used to put valuable items in a secret safe.

He opened the safe and took the other half of the manuscript, smiling with sorrow and talking to himself: "Where are you now? Brown whaler? The clue to your success is in the hands of your grandson now!"

He also saw the two containers that were filled with the soil from B 001. "You two are coming with me too!"

Brown returned to the hospital for Tai. He welcomed him with joy saying: "What did you find, my friend?" Rebecca was there too.

Brown cleared the table in the room and he put the two pieces of the manuscript together and said: "Now what do you see, knight?"

By putting the two pieces together they saw a complete landing zone with a space ship in the middle. The people of Earth were standing on the left side while the ship's riders were standing on the right side.

Tai focused on a symbol in the middle of the landing zone. The symbol was in the shape of a square with special symbols in it.

Tai smiled and said: "This symbol is telling a story of two angel brothers who were always together, until the day they were given the duty of protecting the gates of heaven and hell. The Gods gave the key of heaven to one of them and the key of hell to the other brother, and because of these keys, the brothers never meet again. I think it was for good to tell this story here."

"What do you mean?" Brown asked him.

"I told you, if someone tries to destroy these keys they will send tracking signals to the place they came from."

"That's why I believe Tai Onatem the first knew how to destroy Sattola's keys but he didn't. Instead, he describes how to do that."

"In order to destroy the keys you have to combine them together, and that's why he tells the story of the two angel brothers."

"I will dive my mace in to the shield of the black sun's heart... I will be happy if Fury is back alive!" Rebecca said this with her eyes glowing by the brightness of vengeance!

Tie talked to Rebecca and said: "We appreciate your feelings, Rebecca, however, how do you manage to get close to Fury before you steam away?"

"You will need a shield that can stand against the anti-matter energy."

Brown interrupted: "I think I found something that can help us when I was in the asteroid belt zone and exactly when we discovered the B 001 with the hidden "Black Hole's Heart" deep within. The soil of B 001 has a unique ability."

"And what is that?" Tai asked.

"It has the power to absorb all kinds of energy. They did tons of tests on it in NASA… I don't know why, because it's exposed to a high level of the positron activity that changed the neutron combination of the soil."

Tai said: "Add another reason, the black hole's heart was of small size. Therefore, planet Cateen was not destroyed completely and it left behind the Asteroid belt beside the soil that covered B 001."

I also think because of the transformation due to exposure to energy antimatter B001's soil has acquired this property. Haha, ironically, the soil of the planet that was destroyed will taken the revenge.

"We are lucky, after all we will need a weapon to fight Fury if he comes back," Brown said.

Tai was thinking this time, and then his eyes opened wide and said: "Come with me outside. Brown we have work to do… you too, Rebecca."

Outside Tai was standing and staring at them with no words... they couldn't wait anymore so Brown said: "Hey, Tai, what's wrong with you? Don't let us wait like this... say something!"

"NOW, we have to dedicate a knight to fight Mad Fury so, I decide to choose..."

"YOU WILL NOT CHOOSE ANYONE BUT MEEE!" Rebecca said. "There is big bill on Fury and I'm attempting to make him pay!"

"Rebecca, it's not as easy as you think; there are many tests and hard training that must be passed by the knight... and the most important thing is, controlling the power that will be given to the knight," Tai explained to Rebecca.

"Rebecca, we understand how you feel, but it's a fateful matter. Our enemy is powerful and fearless; he is not going to have mercy on anyone who stands in his way. This knight will be our last hope," Brown said to Rebecca.

"I know all that, I promise you guys my purpose will be defending Earth from the evil and protecting the good people in the universe, and not for vengeance... I promise you."

"Ok then, I will start the preparations for the ceremony. First, I will rise up the level of Rebecca's mind power so she can control the elements of nature. Second, I will start your training on the many ways to fight on the battle field with experience." Tai was talking to Rebecca and hoping she would pass the entire test.

Tai started the ceremony by drawing a big square; inside of the square there was an X letter. At the top part of the square there was triangle.

Then he made four symbols inside the square and he put each one at a corner of the letter X. Then he told Rebecca to sit in the middle of that square. He stood on the top of triangle.

"These symbols stand for the four elements of Earth along with the element of human in the center. NOW! LET US BEGIN!" Tie shouted and the shadows started covering the square. Rebecca closed her eyes and floated in the air unconsciously.

Then the four different colors came down on the four symbols, combined in the center, and became one bright white light.

By dawn, the ceremony was over and Rebecca was ready for stage two.

In stage two, Rebecca started the training for her new fighting skills and yes, she was a very smart student; she learned every technique very fast besides the ability to control her new powers.

"Now you are ready, Rebecca, I can now anoint the birth of a new knight in the galaxy's knight's troop."

Chapter Sixteen

The people of Earth didn't wait for too long before the detection of the ship of Mad Fury on the Earth radars.

This time they didn't know what he was going to do to them. He was pure evil and you couldn't predict what he was going to do.

"There you are again evil face... I thought he died in the explosion."

Fury landed on the Earth like a bolt with a big explosion and he was screaming with scary voice and his eyes shining with death!

"HOW DARE YOU DESTROY EVERYTHING! HUH? WHO DO YOU THINK YOU ARE? DO YOU KNOW HOW MY REVENGE ON YOU WILL LOOK ! YOU WILL TASTE MY WRATH! I WILL ENSLAVE YOUR MISERABLE PLANET FOR ETERNITY! AND YOUR PEOPLE WILL BE MY SLAVES WITH NO ONE TO SAVE YOOOOUUUU! WHO WILL SAVE YOU NOW? WHO?"

"I WILL!" came a strong voice from behind!

Fury turned around to find a female knight riding a horse made from pure white energy. She was covered with golden dust from head to toe, and she had a small white crown on her head too.

"HUH! a new knight I see? You must be from Earth! A NEW VICTIM! Tai must have involved you in this game... go now little one! Run away while you still can!"

Rebecca said: "NO! not before you pay what you owe, YOU DEMON! I will not let you escape this time... there is no mercy for you!"

"HAHAHAHAHAHA! WE WILL SEE WHO ASKS FOR MERCY AND RUNS AWAAAAYYYY!"

Fury covered himself with a field of his energy and shot a big powerful wave on Rebecca.

This time he decided to finish the battle from the beginning with one strike!

However, Rebecca replied in an unexpected way... beyond his imagination! Rebecca's shield took the hit and absorbed the energy like nothing happened!

Rebecca was equipped with the thunder fists... Yo-Zuri's favorite weapon, along with Thunder's chain.

She clashed with Fury in the fight and she hit him more the three times.

Fury took his sword to fight Rebecca with, but the chain of thunder was waiting for him!

She grabbed his sword with her chain and tossed it away then she tied him up with a strong field of energy from her shield.

Then the moment came... she locked up the field on him till he screamed with pain and fell on the ground.

Rebecca sat on his chest, then grabbed her good luck's mace and inserted it in to the black sun's armor. She turned the mace in the other direction and the armor started glowing down little by little.

Finally, she ripped off the black sun and the armor back to its low level just like before!

Now she had him in her hand and he became her prisoner! She had never hurt a creature in her whole life, so she hesitated at first.

Yet then she remembered the thousands of people who had been killed by this criminal's hands. She also remembered her poor beloved grandmother! How heartless he was! She planned for this moment and she imagined the many ways to kill him!

Now he was under her mercy! And yet... she can't make a slight move!

Rebecca's concentration level became a little lower and her fist around the thunder's chain got weaker.

Fury took this chance and pull up his feet around Rebecca's neck trying to break it or knock her on the ground.

Rebecca was back to her consciousness and moved along with him without any resistance, and that was for a purpose!

She threw herself back and relayed on his legs with her shoulders! Then she pulled up her entire body in the air, vertically, and... BBAAAMM! She went down with all her strength on his chest... WITH HER ANKLE!

Fury shouted with severe pain and fell on his back while Rebecca stood again on his chest!

This time she didn't give him a second… "TAKE THIS! IT'S FOR YOU FROM MY GRANDMOTHER! WITH LOVE!"

She was carrying her grandma's favorite knife in her belt! Her grandma used to cut meat with this knife.

It was a very sharp knife with a short blade; one of the red Indians gave it to her grandfather Zuckerberg.

Rebecca stabbed Fury with her knife in his forehead and broke the handle to leave the blade inside his head!

So the end of MAD FURY finally came true! It was fast and inevitable!

The cry of victory went high in the sky from all people of Earth!

The nightmare of Fury and his ghosts were over now.

The people of Earth started rebuilding what was destroyed by the hands of the evil Fury. Tai gained his strength back after a few months and he started to get ready for his return. His ship was fixed and was ready to travel.

"This will be an epic story to tell for the next generations in our galaxy. You ended a nightmare that stayed for millions of years. And it's became a heroic tale to be told, please feel free to come and visit anytime you like!" Tai said.

"Of course we will!" Brown said. "We must communicate to gain experience and science from an advanced people like you!"

"See you later my good friends!" Brown said to Tai.

Tai's ship flew away and everybody waved their hands for him.

Rebecca smiled to Brown and said: "I have to go now, Brown... I have to re-build my grandfather's store; I will continue my way alone!"

Brown grabbed her in his arms and said with a gentle voice: "You will not be alone... I promise you!"

THE END

www.ingramcontent.com/pod-product-compliance
Lightning Source LLC
LaVergne TN
LVHW091604060526
838200LV00036B/984